FIRST POPULAR PIECES
FOR THE FLUTE

ARRANGED BY ROBIN DE SMET

Wise Publications
London/New York/Sydney

4.95

Exclusive Distributors:
Music Sales Limited
8/9 Frith Street, London, W1V 5TZ, England.

Music Sales Pty. Limited
120 Rothschild Avenue, Rosebery, NSW 2018, Australia.

This book © Copyright 1986 by
Wise Publications
UK ISBN 0.7119.0739.0
UK Order No. AM 60328

Designed by Howard Brown
Arranged and compiled by Robin De Smet

Music Sales complete catalogue lists thousands of
titles and is free from your local music shop,
or direct from Music Sales Limited.
Please send a cheque or Postal Order
for £1.50 for postage to
Music Sales Limited, 8/9 Frith Street, London, W1V 5TZ.

Printed in England by
J.B. Offset Printers (Marks Tey) Limited, Marks Tey.

AFTER THE BALL

WORDS & MUSIC BY CHARLES K. HARRIS

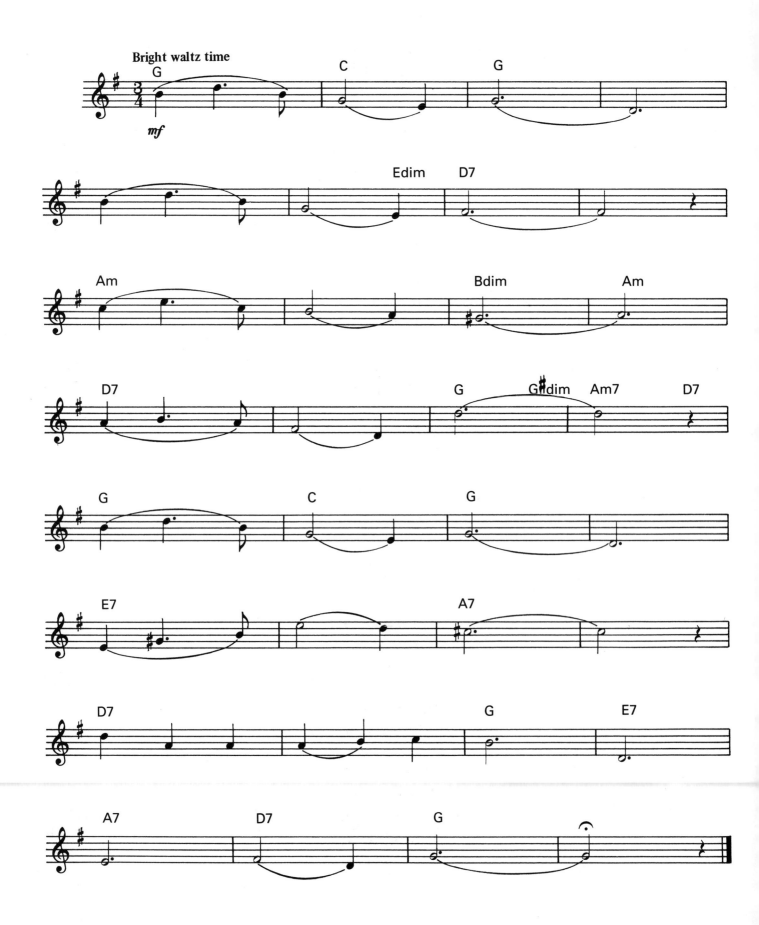

ALL MY LOVING

WORDS & MUSIC BY
JOHN LENNON & PAUL McCARTNEY

AMAZING GRACE

TRADITIONAL

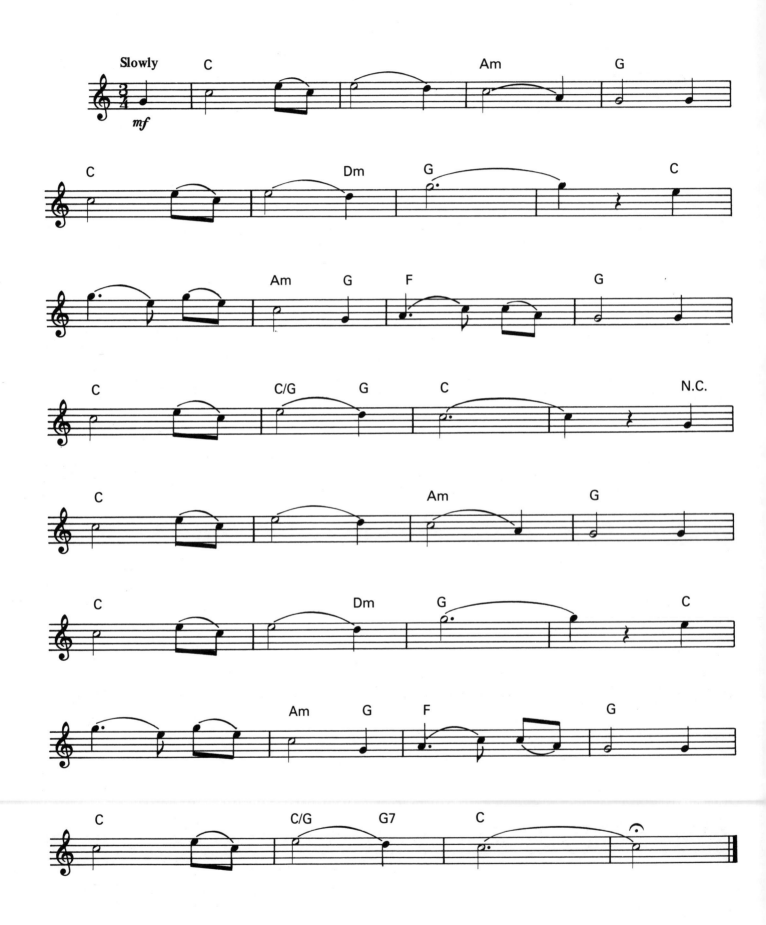

AS LONG AS HE NEEDS ME

WORDS & MUSIC BY LIONEL BART

THE BALLAD OF DAVY CROCKETT

WORDS BY TOM BLACKBURN
MUSIC BY GEORGE BRUNS

DANNY BOY ('Londonderry Air')

WORDS BY FRED E. WEATHERLY
MUSIC: TRADITIONAL IRISH MELODY

DO-RE-MI

WORDS BY OSCAR HAMMERSTEIN II
MUSIC BY RICHARD RODGERS

EDELWEISS

WORDS BY OSCAR HAMMERSTEIN II
MUSIC BY RICHARD RODGERS

Slowly with expression

GREENSLEEVES

TRADITIONAL

IN THE GOOD OLD SUMMERTIME

WORDS BY REN SHIELDS
MUSIC BY GEORGE EVANS

KARMA CHAMELEON

WORDS & MUSIC BY
O'DOWD, MOSS, HAY, CRAIG & PICKETT

LARGO ('From The New World')

BY ANTONIN DVORAK

LITTLE BROWN JUG

TRADITIONAL

LOVE IS A SONG

WORDS BY LARRY MOREY
MUSIC BY FRANK CHURCHILL

LOVE ME TENDER

WORDS & MUSIC BY
ELVIS PRESLEY & VERA MATSON

MICHELLE

WORDS & MUSIC BY
JOHN LENNON & PAUL McCARTNEY

NELLIE THE ELEPHANT

WORDS BY RALPH BUTLER
MUSIC BY PETER HART

NEVER WEATHERBEATEN SAIL

BY THOMAS CAMPION

NORWEGIAN WOOD

WORDS & MUSIC BY
JOHN LENNON & PAUL McCARTNEY

OH! SUSANNA

WORDS & MUSIC BY STEPHEN FOSTER

ON THE CREST OF A WAVE

WORDS & MUSIC BY RALPH READER

O SOLE MIO

BY E. DI CAPUA

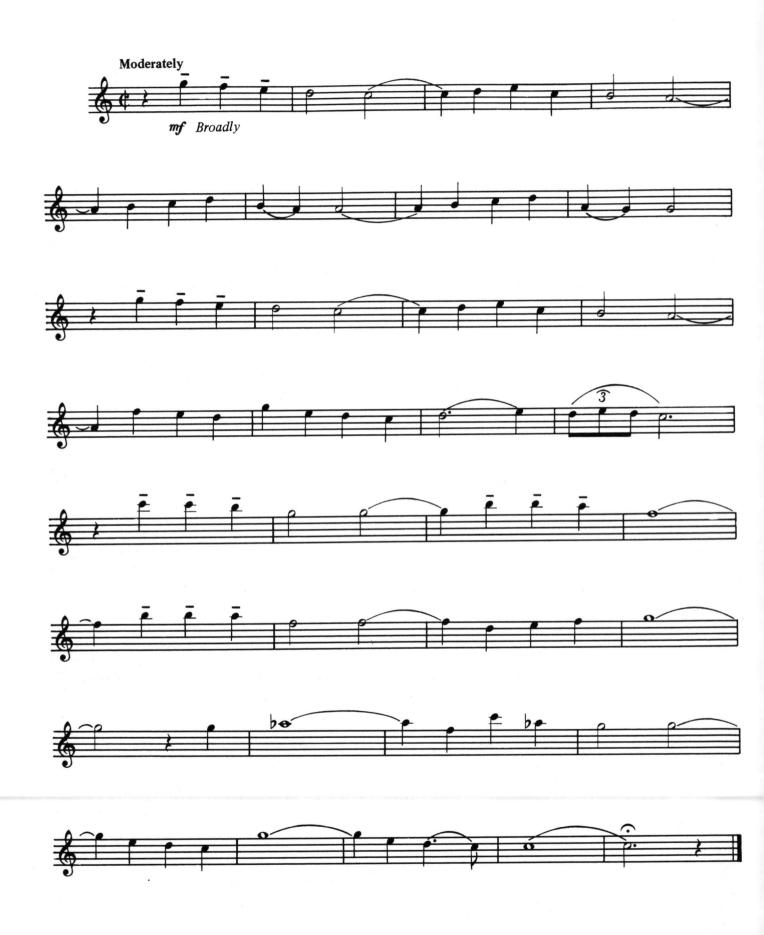

SAILING

WORDS & MUSIC BY GAVIN SUTHERLAND

SHENANDOAH

TRADITIONAL

SMILE

WORDS BY JOHN TURNER & GEOFFREY PARSONS
MUSIC BY CHARLES CHAPLIN

STREETS OF LONDON

WORDS & MUSIC BY RALPH McTELL

SUMER IS ICUMEN IN

ANONYMOUS

[A Round In Four Parts]

SUNRISE SUNSET

WORDS BY SHELDON HARNICK
MUSIC BY JERRY BOCK

SWEET ROSIE O'GRADY

WORDS & MUSIC BY MAUDE NUGENT

TOO YOUNG

WORDS BY SYLVIA DEE
MUSIC BY SID LIPPMAN

TRULY SCRUMPTIOUS

WORDS & MUSIC BY
RICHARD M. SHERMAN & ROBERT B. SHERMAN

TULIPS FROM AMSTERDAM

ENGLISH WORDS BY GENE MARTYN
ORIGINAL WORDS BY NEUMANN BADER
MUSIC BY RALF ARNIE

THE WILLOW SONG

ANON

WITH A LITTLE HELP FROM MY FRIENDS

WORDS & MUSIC BY
JOHN LENNON & PAUL McCARTNEY

WOODEN HEART

WORDS & MUSIC BY
FRED WISE, BEN WEISMAN, KAY TWOMEY & BERTHOLD KAEMPFERT

THE YELLOW ROSE OF TEXAS

Traditional

YOU NEED HANDS

WORDS & MUSIC BY MAX BYGRAVES

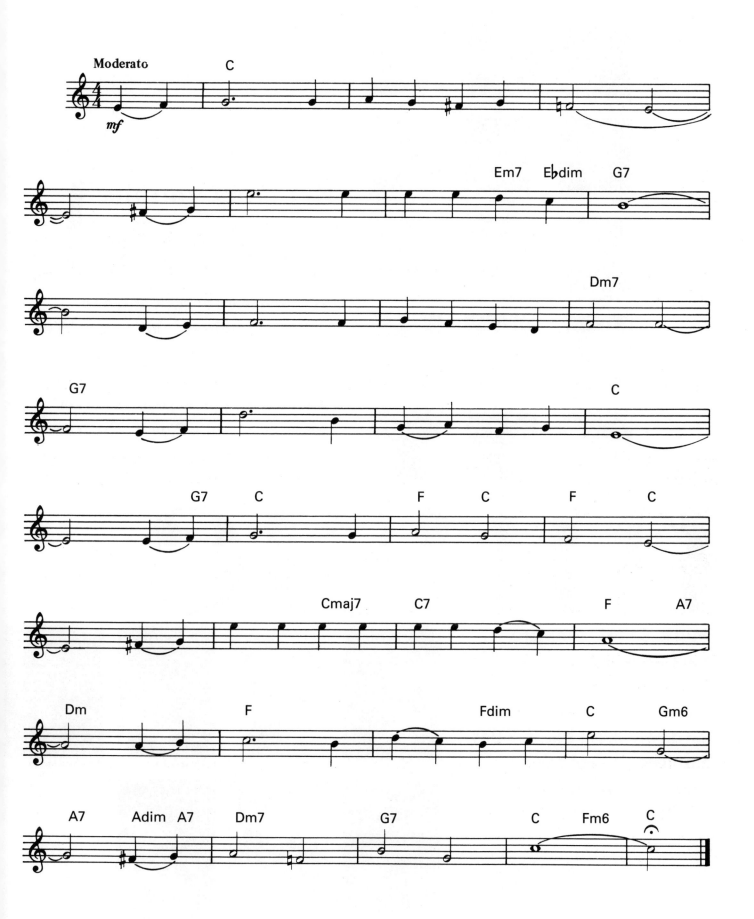

The Beatles

Enya

Phil Collins

Van Morrison

Bob Dylan

Sting

Paul Simon

Tracy Chapman

Eric Clapton

Pink Floyd

New Kids On The Block

Bringing you the words

**All the latest in rock and pop.
Plus the brightest and best in West
End show scores. Music books for
every instrument under the sun.
And exciting new teach-yourself
ideas like "Let's Play Keyboard" -
in cassette/book packs, or on video.
Available from all good music shops.**

Bryan Adams

Tina Turner

Elton John

and

Bee Gees

Whitney Houston

AC/DC

music

**Music Sales' complete
catalogue lists thousands of
titles and is available free
from your local music shop,
or direct from Music Sales
Limited. Please send a
cheque or postal order for
£1.50 (for postage) to:**

Music Sales Limited
Newmarket Road,
Bury St Edmunds,
Suffolk IP33 3YB

Buddy

Five Guys Named Moe

Les Misérables

West Side Story

Phantom Of The Opera

Show Boat

The Rocky Horror Show

**Bringing you the
world's best music.**